Night-Night, Poppy!

Claire Freedman

Jane Massey

LITTLE TIGER PRESS
London

It was bedtime, but Poppy couldn't find her favourite bear, Growly Ted. She'd looked everywhere.

Mummy had to tuck her in
with Quacky Duck instead.
  "Night-night, Poppy, night-night,
Quacky Duck," said Mummy.
  "Night-night, Mummy and
Quacky Duck," said Poppy.
  "Quack-quack!" quacked
Quacky Duck.

Poppy would have fallen fast
asleep right then. But OH NO!
The bed didn't feel quite right.
So Poppy went to find Furry Cat.

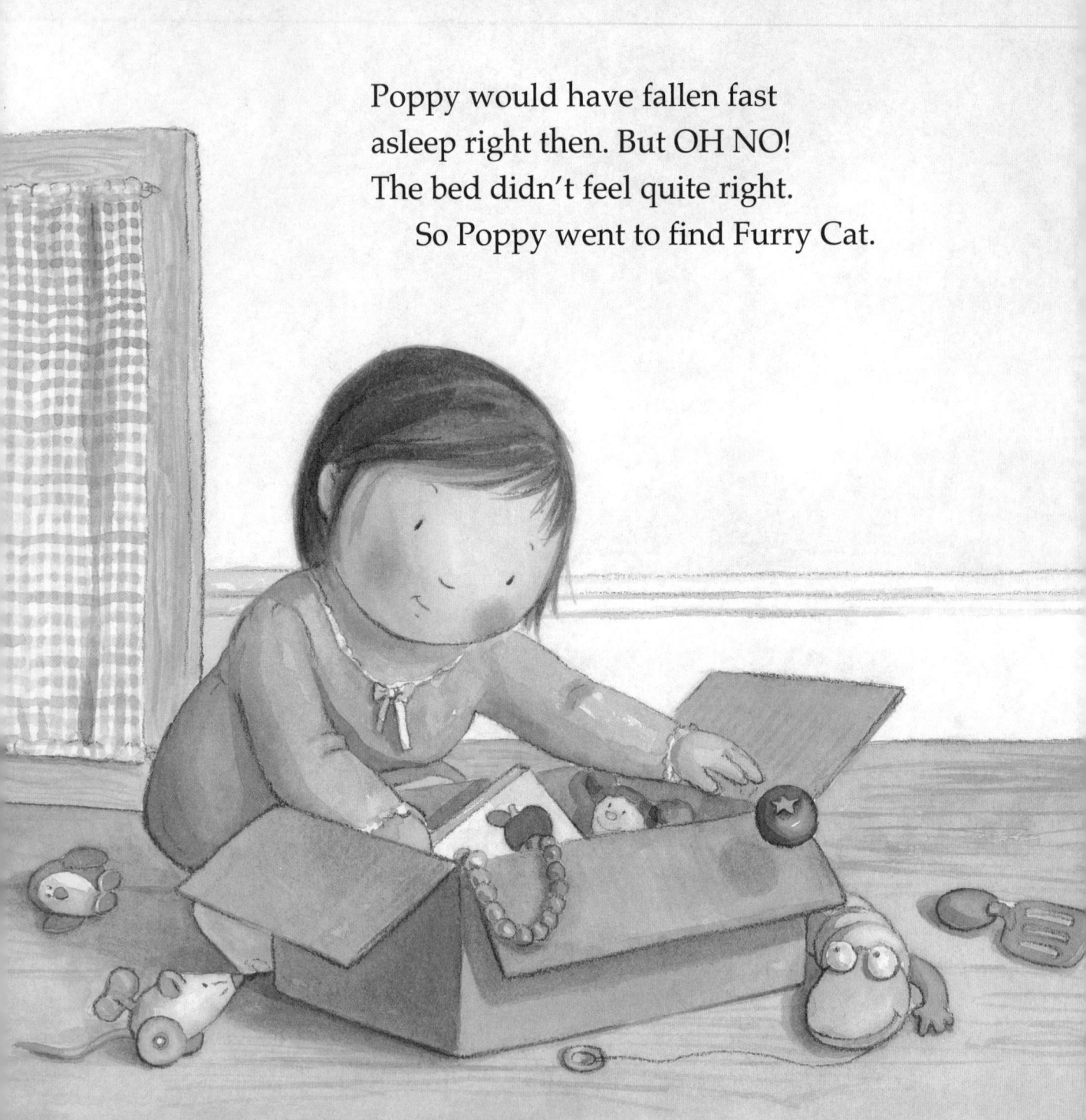

"Night-night, Quacky Duck and Furry Cat,"
said Poppy.
"Miaow," purred Furry Cat.
"Quack-quack," quacked Quacky Duck.

Poppy would have fallen fast asleep that
very minute. But OH NO! The bed STILL
didn't feel quite right. It felt too empty.
    Out Poppy climbed to look for Hooty Owl.

"Night-night," Poppy told Hooty Owl, Furry Cat and Quacky Duck.

"Too-whit, too-whoo," hooted Hooty Owl.

"Miaow," purred Furry Cat.

"Quack-quack," quacked Quacky Duck. "Quack!"

Poppy would have fallen asleep in a flash.
But OH NO! Now the bed felt too draughty.
   Where had Dimple Dog got to?
   Poppy found him downstairs, behind the curtains.

"Night-night, Dimple Dog and
Hooty Owl," said Poppy.
"Night-night, Furry Cat and
Quacky Duck."
    "Woof-woof," barked Dimple Dog.
    "Too-whit, too-whoo," hooted
Hooty Owl.
    "Miaow," purred Furry Cat.
    Quacky Duck didn't say a word.
He was already fast asleep.

Poppy would have fallen fast asleep too.
But OH NO! Now the bed covers felt too loose.
Poppy crept out to find Woolly Lamb.

"Night-night, everyone," said Poppy.
  "Baa-baa," bleated Woolly Lamb.
  "Woof-woof," barked Dimple Dog.
  "Too-whit, too-whoo," hooted
Hooty Owl.
  "Miaow," purred Furry Cat.
  "Quack-quack," quacked Quacky Duck,
who'd woken up again with all the noise.

Now Poppy would have fallen fast
asleep in an instant. But OH NO!
She just couldn't get comfy.
The pillow felt all lumpy.

"What's under here?" said Poppy.
"Oh, so that's where you've been
hiding, silly Growly Ted!"

Then Poppy put
Quacky Duck
back in the toy box.

She propped
Furry Cat back
up on his shelf.

She put Hooty Owl
back under
the bed.

And she carried
Dimple Dog
and Woolly Lamb
back downstairs.

Then Poppy and Growly Ted settled
down together under the covers.
"Night-night, Growly Ted,"
yawned Poppy.
"Grrr!" growled Growly Ted.
And Poppy fell fast asleep.
OH YES! Because the bed felt
just right.

And Growly Ted
would have fallen fast asleep
that same second too.
But OH NO! . . .

Suddenly the bed
was far too full!
"Grrrr!"

For my good friend Elaine
~ C F

For Grandma, with love
~ J M

LITTLE TIGER PRESS
1 The Coda Centre, 189 Munster Road, London SW6 6AW
www.littletiger.co.uk

First published in Great Britain 2003
This edition published 2012

Printed in China • LTP/1800/0794/0913

4 6 8 10 9 7 5 3